Farm Fun

Farm Plants

by Tessa Kenan

Bullfrog Books

Ideas for Parents and Teachers

Bullfrog Books let children practice reading informational text at the earliest reading levels. Repetition, familiar words, and photo labels support early readers.

Before Reading

- Discuss the cover photo. What does it tell them?
- Look at the picture glossary together. Read and discuss the words.

Read the Book

- "Walk" through the book and look at the pictures. Let the child ask questions. Point out the photo labels.
- Read the book to the child, or have him or her read independently.

After Reading

- Prompt the child to think more. Ask: Many crops grow on farms. Have you seen a field of crops before? Do you know what crop it was?

Bullfrog Books are published by Jump!
5357 Penn Avenue South
Minneapolis, MN 55419
www.jumplibrary.com

Library of Congress Cataloging-in-Publication Data

Names: Kenan, Tessa, author.
Title: Farm plants / by Tessa Kenan.
Description: Minneapolis, MN: Jump!, Inc., [2021].
Series: Farm fun | Includes index.
Identifiers: LCCN 2019053339 (print)
LCCN 2019053340 (ebook)
ISBN 9781645275275 (hardcover)
ISBN 9781645275282 (ebook)
Subjects: LCSH: Food crops—United States—
Juvenile literature. | Food crops—Juvenile literature.
Farm produce—United States—Juvenile literature.
Farm produce—Juvenile literature.
Classification: LCC SB176.U6 K46 2021 (print)
LCC SB176.U6 (ebook) | DDC 630.973—dc23
LC record available at https://lccn.loc.gov/2019053339
LC ebook record available at https://lccn.loc .gov/2019053340

Editor: Jenna Gleisner
Designer: David Stavitzski

Photo Credits: Mr.Rawin Tainpin/Shutterstock, cover; Maks Narodenko/Shutterstock, 1; robertsre/Shutterstock, 3; Velychko/Shutterstock, 4; robert cicchetti/Shutterstock, 5, 22tl, 23tl; oticki/Shutterstock, 6–7, 9, 22bl; Luis Carlos Jimenez del rio/Shutterstock, 8; Ievgenii Meyer/Shutterstock, 10–11, 22br; Valentyn Volkov/Shutterstock, 12–13; blisser/Shutterstock, 14–15, 23bl; Production Perig/Shutterstock, 16–17 (foreground); Phil Darby/Shutterstock, 16–17 (background); Rawpixel.com/Shutterstock, 18, 23tr; Elena Elisseeva/Shutterstock, 19; Adisa/Shutterstock, 20–21; muratart/Shutterstock, 22tr; marcin jucha/Shutterstock, 23br; Ramon L. Farinos/Shutterstock, 24.

Printed in the United States of America at Corporate Graphics in North Mankato, Minnesota.

Table of Contents

Farm Food

Where does most of our food come from?

Farms!

Farmers plant many crops.
Corn is one. See the stalks?

rows

Soybeans grow in rows.

Neat!

What are these? Sugar beets!

They grow in rows, too.

This is wheat.
It is gold.

Crops are made into the foods we eat.

Cool!

Some crops become food for animals.

Hay is one.

Cows eat it!

hay

Many farms have gardens, too!

Vegetables grow in them.

So do herbs.

Cool!

Farmers sell them. Where?

Farmer's markets!

We eat fresh food.

Yum!

Many plants grow on farms!

What is your favorite?

Top Crops

These are some of the most popular crops grown in the United States.

Picture Glossary

crops
Plants grown for food.

farmer's markets
Markets at which local farmers sell their agriculture products directly to buyers.

hay
Long grass that is dried and used as food for farm animals.

herbs
Plants or parts of plants that are used in cooking or medicine.

Index

To Learn More

Finding more information is as easy as 1, 2, 3.

1. Go to www.factsurfer.com
2. Enter "farmplants" into the search box.
3. Click the "Surf" button to see a list of websites.